Curious George

by

H. A. Rey

Houghton Mifflin Company, Boston

Printed in the United States of America

ISBN: 0-395-15993-8 Reinforced Edition
ISBN: 0-395-15023-X Sandpiper Edition

WOZ **Sixty Ninth Printing**

This book belongs to

My Lean

This is George.
He lived in Africa.
He was a good little monkey
and always very curious.

One day George saw a man.
He had on a large yellow straw hat.
The man saw George too.
"What a nice little monkey," he thought.
"I would like to take him home with me."
He put his hat on the ground
and, of course, George was curious.
He came down from the tree
to look at the large yellow hat.

The hat had been on the man's head.
George thought it would be nice
to have it on his own head.
He picked it up and put it on.

The hat covered George's head.
He couldn't see.
The man picked him up quickly
and popped him into a bag.
George was caught.

The man with the big yellow hat
put George into a little boat,
and a sailor rowed them both
across the water to a big ship.
George was sad, but he was still
a little curious.

On the big ship, things began to happen.
The man took off the bag.
George sat on a little stool and the man said,
"George, I am going to take you to a big Zoo
in a big city. You will like it there.
Now run along and play,
but don't get into trouble."
George promised to be good.
But it is easy for little monkeys to forget.

On the deck he found some sea gulls.
He wondered how they could fly.
He was very curious.
Finally he HAD to try.
It looked easy. But—

oh, what happened!
First this—

and then this!

"WHERE IS GEORGE?"
The sailors looked and looked.
At last they saw him
struggling in the water,
and almost all tired out.

"Man overboard!" the sailors cried
as they threw him a lifebelt.
George caught it and held on.
At last he was safe on board.

After that George was more careful
to be a good monkey, until, at last,
the long trip was over.
George said good-bye to the kind sailors,
and he and the man with the yellow hat
walked off the ship on to the shore
and on into the city to the man's house.

After a good meal
and a good pipe
George felt very tired.

He crawled into bed
and fell asleep at once.

The next morning
the man telephoned the Zoo.
George watched him.
He was fascinated.
Then the man went away.

George was curious.
He wanted to telephone, too.
One, two, three, four, five, six, seven.
What fun!

DING-A-LING-A-LING!
GEORGE HAD TELEPHONED
THE FIRE STATION!
The firemen rushed to the telephone.
"Hello! Hello!" they said.
But there was no answer.
Then they looked for the signal
on the big map that showed
where the telephone call had come from.
They didn't know it was GEORGE.
They thought it was a real fire.

HURRY! HURRY! HURRY!
The firemen jumped on to the fire engines
and on to the hook-and-ladders.
Ding-dong-ding-dong.
Everyone out of the way!
Hurry! Hurry! Hurry!

The firemen rushed into the house.

They opened the door.

NO FIRE!

ONLY a naughty little monkey.

"Oh, catch him, catch him," they cried.

George tried to run away.

He almost did, but he got caught

in the telephone wire, and—

a thin fireman caught one arm
and a fat fireman caught the other.
"You fooled the fire department,"
they said. "We will have to shut you up
where you can't do any more harm."
They took him away
and shut him in a prison.

George wanted to get out.
He climbed up to the window
to try the bars.
Just then the watchman came in.
He got on the wooden bed to catch George.
But he was too big and heavy.
The bed tipped up,
the watchman fell over,
and, quick as lightning,
George ran out through the open door.

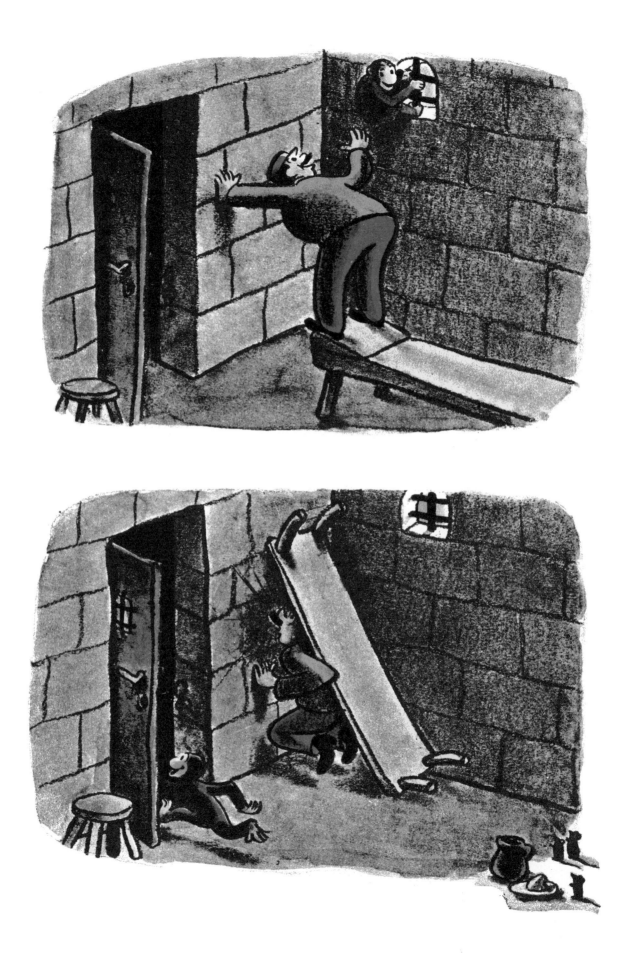

He hurried through the building
and out on to the roof. And then
he was lucky to be a monkey:
out he walked on to the telephone wires.
Quickly and quietly over the guard's head,
George walked away.
He was free!

Down in the street
outside the prison wall,
stood a balloon man.
A little girl bought a balloon
for her brother.
George watched.
He was curious again.
He felt he MUST have
a bright red balloon.
He reached over and
tried to help himself, but—

instead of one balloon,
the whole bunch broke loose.
In an instant
the wind whisked them all away
and, with them, went George,
holding tight with both hands.

Up, up he sailed, higher and higher.
The houses looked like toy houses
and the people like dolls.
George was frightened.
He held on very tight.

At first the wind blew in great gusts.
Then it quieted.
Finally it stopped blowing altogether.
George was very tired.
Down, down he went—bump,
on to the top of a traffic light.
Everyone was surprised.
The traffic got all mixed up.
George didn't know what to do,
and then he heard someone call,
"GEORGE!"
He looked down and saw his friend,
the man with the big yellow hat!

George was very happy.
The man was happy too.
George slid down the post
and the man with the big yellow hat
put him under his arm.
Then he paid the balloon man
for all the balloons.
And then George and the man
climbed into the car
and at last, away they went

to the ZOO!

What a nice place
for George to live!